accidentally inn love

ABBY KNOX

Copyright © 2022 by Abby Knox

All rights reserved.

No part of this book may be reproduced in any form or by any electronic or mechanical means, including information storage and retrieval systems, without written permission from the author, except for the use of brief quotations in a book review.

Publisher's Note: This is a work of fiction. Names, characters, places, and incidents are a product of the author's imagination. Locales and public names are sometimes used for atmospheric purposes. Any resemblance to actual people, living or dead, or to businesses, companies, events, institutions, or locales is coincidental.

Edited by Aquila Editing

Cover Designer: Cover Girl Designs

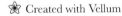 Created with Vellum

Summary

Naomi
I have never experienced such a demanding guest in all my years of running a successful inn. While most tourists understand the quirkiness of an old building, a certain cocky young artist, Caleb, has nothing but complaints about every minor inconvenience. Just when I think I've finally got him settled in, though, things start to go truly haywire. I'm starting to suspect he's inventing problems with his room, just to waste my time and mess with me because he's having some kind of artistic block. He'll soon find out I'm not a woman to be messed with.

Caleb
Naomi is my muse. I knew it the moment she checked me in to my room at this quaint old inn. I came here for a change of scenery and inspiration, but wasn't prepared for her. The only problem now is I don't want to be left alone to work on my art. I want to paint her. Need to paint her. More than that, I need her near me as much as possible. She may be too busy running an inn to sit and model for

me, but I've got bigger plans. And those plans do not involve checking out of this inn anytime soon.

I am so excited to be a part of this group of authors who decided to celebrate International Women's Day all month long by bringing you a sassy, sexy collection of women finding true love with their hot, younger men.

Check out the series here: https://amzn.to/3udqkws

Chapter One

Caleb

I STARE at this blank canvas, but nothing is coming to me.

I had thought that a change of scenery from my tiny one-bedroom condo in the city would help. Maybe spark an idea.

When I found this charming colonial-style inn online, it seemed like the perfect place. Small town, lots of trees, a lake, and rolling hills.

Plus the name: Fate. Seems like a perfect spot to create my masterpiece. Or anything at all.

Upon arrival, the entire town took me by surprise. The bustling downtown square had a brewpub, a couple of cozy restaurants, a yarn store, an art gallery, old factories remodeled into shops, offices, apartments, and performing arts centers. Fate really had me at "Home of the world's largest ball of yarn." That exhibit on the bustling square led me to pick up a brochure for The Curiosity Spot, which turned out to be a modest hill in some farmer's backyard, which threw off my phone compass a bit. The woman running the gift shop had quite a gift of gab. She reminded me of my grandmother, so I bought six souvenir shot glasses that I did not need.

You would think all that exploration would spark something. Or at least help me relax my racing, unproductive thoughts. Why wouldn't it? Everything around me is charming and wholesome as fuck.

Something is wrong with me.

My room, and its view, is the icing on the cake. I have a balcony overlooking the hills and the lake in the distance. It has enough room for my canvas, a chair, and a table with my painting supplies. Straight underneath my balcony is an herb garden. I can smell the rosemary.

And yet here I sit, uninspired.

Who am I kidding? I know exactly what the problem is.

There's nothing wrong with this inn, the view, balcony, or this charming town, or my brushes or paints.

The problem is with the owner of this inn.

When I stare at my canvas, all I see is her face.

Naomi.

Even her name is like a song.

And that's a problem. I don't paint people, especially not faces. I do still lifes, landscapes. Animals. Abstract. I don't do the human form. I've never been able to get them just right.

But something about her, Naomi, makes me want to paint her.

Her easy smile and accent hit me first.

"Welcome to the Braeburn Inn. What can I do for you?"

Already, I'd felt a stirring in my lower half. Shit. Bad timing for a hard-on.

A temporary brain fog occurred—a hazy pink fog with

her being the only thing not blurry in my world—and I forgot what I was doing there.

"Baxter, Caleb," was all I'd managed to say. Like I was reading the phone book.

She'd squinted then, assessing me. My stature? My character? Who knows what secret magical powers she possessed to size me up. Then, she'd smiled and flipped through an ancient-looking leather-bound datebook.

Babbling to fill the silence, I'd corrected myself. "I mean Caleb Baxter, my last name is Baxter. I have a reservation. I should have started with that."

She'd smiled mischievously, and my body responded with a twitching in my drawers. I was a goner. "Oh, I know who you are."

Those six words sent me. That had been the moment I'd been waiting for, for my entire career as an artist.

"You do? Where have you seen my work?"

The confusion on her face told me I'd made yet another mistake.

"Oh no, sweetie. I remember you from when you booked over the phone. It was such a unique name, that's all."

"Oh. Right. Sorry." I could feel my face flood with heat. And yet, my stirring cock didn't flag one bit. In fact, the longer we talked, the harder I became. My outright humiliation did not matter; my need to be in her presence outweighed all sense of self-preservation.

"And where exactly would I have seen your work, Caleb?"

I should never go out in public. I should have turned tail and left right then. I'd wanted to crawl under a bridge and talk to the birds for the rest of my life because I did not want to go on with that interaction. Except, I was transfixed. Frozen to the spot.

So, I doubled down on my egotistical artist persona, like an asshole. I named a few of the spaces and galleries that featured my work. Plus, my alma mater, which still displayed in a dark corner several of my dust-covered paintings that had won national awards. And, of course, the kicker—a slowly growing portfolio of public murals commissioned by a handful of small cities.

Naomi had only nodded, biting her bottom lip in a way that made my insides feel like the floor was dropping out from under me.

"I'm sorry, sweetie. I don't know much about art."

I laughed. "Sometimes, neither do I."

The light chuckle that escaped her was like a caress across my skin. "Well, you're carrying many artistic-looking things with you, so you're already way ahead of me, darlin'."

Oh my god, the terms of endearment were too much. Her accent dripped with it, like sweet tea. I would have married her immediately.

Her gaze raked over my chest and then back up to meet my stare. She's stunning, with her blonde-turning-white hair, dancing friendly eyes, and glittering dangly earrings.

That face is still burned into my brain while I'm on this picturesque balcony, staring at a blank canvas with a brush in one hand and a whiskey in the other to calm my nerves.

Nothing is coming to me. Nothing, except the fiercest erection of all time.

Cursing, I stand up and pace around the room, trying to get Naomi out of my head.

Thinking of how I can possibly get on with my painting.

I plop down on the bed, the springs squeaking loudly against my weight. I press the pads of my fingers into my eyelids as if that might reset my mind to factory settings. The bed noise brings to mind a fun bout of frisky hotel sex, which puts even more thoughts in my head about Naomi.

My hand slides up under my shirt, caressing my lower stomach. God, these thoughts have now entered the zone of inappropriate. My hand slides down lower, and I'm unzipping my jeans before I know it.

Naomi would be horrified, but a quick yank might help clear my head.

Reaching my opposite hand above my head, I grip one of the posts on the antique brass headboard.

Sighing, I shove down the waistband of my boxer briefs, freeing my overheated cock. It slaps against my abdomen, the tiny drop of precum already making a showing, a small splattering against my skin.

"Fuck me," I grit out angrily. I hadn't planned ahead for this, and I don't have any lotion, lube, anything. So, I do the only thing I can do: slather my palm with my own saliva.

My grip on the cold metal contrasts with the hot, rigid pipe in my other hand as I slide my fist up and down.

All rational thought leaks out of my head and is replaced by the vision of her face. The purse of her lips, the sweet laugh lines around her eyes. The curve of her neck, the way her wispy hair frames her face, and her accent. Damn that accent.

Fisting my shaft, I pump hard. The quicker I get this over with, the quicker I can get clear my head to make room for my art. The more I move up and down on my dick, the clearer the picture of her becomes in my head.

Those glistening lips… I can see them wrapped around me.

Cursing and pumping. Pumping and cursing.

Soon, I'm pumping myself so hard and angrily that the bed begins to squeak rhythmically. A remnant of rational thought crosses my mind—I don't want to break the bedsprings. I grip the bedpost tighter and try to go slower and calmer.

But dammit, I don't want to go slow. I need to go hard and fast. As soon as I slow down, it feels like I'm edging myself, and I nearly crack my teeth in frustration. I need to come. I just need to come.

So I just do it. I pump again and again and again until I'm spraying into her sweet mouth. In my stupid juvenile fantasy, I come down her throat, and she swallows. As I roar out my orgasm, I pull hard on the bedframe. And the brass post I'm gripping snaps off in my hand.

"Fuck!"

I've been here 20 minutes, and I'm already breaking the furniture.

Sitting up, I curse again and wipe the jizz off my stomach with the tail of my shirt.

The odd mixture of relief and shame washes over me.

Until I realize I have a perfect excuse to see her again.

Chapter Two

Naomi

It's Caleb's room calling the front desk. I pick up the extension.

"How can I help you, Mr. Baxter?"

"Yeah…uh…there's a problem with the bed frame that I think you should look at."

That's odd. I checked everything over with the room after the cleaning crew had been through. I can't imagine what he would be complaining about.

When I arrive at his room, Caleb opens the door looking flushed and out of sorts, but weirdly relaxed.

"You said something about the bedframe?"

He leads me to the bed, and I examine it, seeing nothing wrong at first. Then, he hands me a long thin cylinder of brass. I look at the metal, warm from his touch. And then I look back up at Caleb quizzically.

"The bedpost broke," he says quickly.

What I'd thought was a broken frame turns out to be a broken post on the headboard.

"How?"

The flush in his young cheeks deepens. He shrugs. "I don't know. I was taking a break from my painting, and I went to lie down. Next thing I know, thffft." He makes this noise with his tongue as if that explains everything.

Something is off about this. There's something he's not telling me. So I decide to fuck with him. "Mr. Baxter, what did you do to my grandma's antique bed?"

The pink in his cheeks drains as he blanches. "Your… grandmother's bed?"

I cross my arms in disgust. "Were you entertaining a lady friend?"

He stammers, the poor thing. "A what? N-no!"

"Because the inn policy clearly states that no third party visitors are allowed up here. No parties, no guests unaccounted for. If you plan on bedding someone, that's your business, but every visitor must be accounted for."

His eyes widen, and he shows me his palms. "I would never do that in your inn, ma'am."

"This is not a pay-by-the-hour no-tell motel, sir," I say.

Caleb rubs a hand through his hair. "I know, I know. That's not…that's the last thing I would ever want you of all people to think I was doing up here."

What a strange thing to say. I squint at him.

"Please don't kick me out."

I have no intention of kicking him out. He's pre-paid for a month, even pre-paid a massive tip for the cleaning crew and the wait staff at the restaurant. Unless he turns out to be a war criminal, he can stay as long as he wants.

But I'm still not done fucking with him. He's so young and good-looking and full of himself, and I've got him on the ropes.

I can't keep doing this. I let go of the fake tension in my face and smile. "I'm sorry. I was messing with you. It's not my grandmother's bed."

"It's not?"

I shake my head, laughing. "I'm so sorry, but the look on your face was too much. I shouldn't have done that."

He waves off my apology, blowing out a breath. "That's a relief. I was worried that your grandmother's ghost would haunt me for breaking her bed."

Taking the brass post in my fist, I start to work on the headboard. "I should be able to pop this back into place. But you have to try to remember this is an old building. It's going to have its quirks. If you can't live with something being imperfect, like a headboard decoration, I just ask that you write me a note instead of asking me to come up. I can fix things, but I'm short-handed this weekend. My handyman is out of town."

Perhaps that was a little too bristly because he says, "I'm sorry to pull you away from the more important stuff. My apologies."

When I finish and turn to leave, Caleb is standing in front of his canvas out on the balcony, and I see three smooth lines of black that he's brushed on. His face is full of concentration, but it's not on the project. His eyes are trained right on me.

He looks at me like a person who doesn't realize that their subject is staring right back at them, as if he doesn't realize how unsettling he is.

For a brief moment, I let his deep eyes survey me. He seems to be looking at my arms, which are bare in this silk shirt I'm wearing. When other guests stare at me like this, it usually sends me diving for my blazer to cover up. This man, however. There's something so unmasked about his face, like someone in a state of flow. Whether he's staring at my shoulder or my collarbone, I don't care. But it has the same effect as it would if he were staring straight at my breasts.

My nipples bloom into stiff peaks under my bra, making me wish I had worn something other than a flimsy lace thing today. My smallish tits and unruly nipples make working in silk and chiffon a risk. There's no telling when they might decide to make an appearance.

As if some otherworldly energy is at play, I choose to let him stare rather than cover up with my blazer.

He blinks, his lips parted in concentration. My eyes fall to his hands, those long, lean fingers rolling the paintbrush back and forth. The slow movement of those agile fingertips sends my mind reeling. And I like what I see on the canvas. It's fresh and different and captures me in an unexpected kind of way. I feel heated everywhere.

What is the matter with me? He's got to be fifteen years my junior. Not even in my same generation, for Pete's sake. Gen Xers are not supposed to be fascinated by millennials, are they? We're supposed to be jaded as fuck.

Gathering the sense that I was born with, I clear my throat. "I'd better go. Lots to do. Enjoy your afternoon, and I'll see you at dinner."

His voice is low and craggy but soft. "If not sooner."

An unnerving wave of emotion rolls over me as I make my way down the long carpeted hallway with my toolbox. It's a feeling of something unearthed that should not have been dug up. Horniness. That's all it is, Naomi.

I sigh and swallow hard before knocking on the door of room 2B. Mrs. Maxwell has a leaky faucet. Thank god for her clipped sentences and those nauseating fox stoles of hers resting on the bed; everything about Mrs. Maxwell clears away any lusty fantasies in my head, allowing me to focus on the job.

"You really ought to hire a handyman," she says.

"Donovan's out of the country with his wife and kids," I say. As my most frequent guest, I would have thought the Gold Hill matriarch would have the staff's annual schedules memorized by now. Donovan always takes two weeks in April to travel with his family. He was one of my first hires when I started fixing up this old inn, and he's now worked with me for well over seven years.

Mrs. Maxwell clucks her tongue. "If your staff can afford long vacations, you're paying them too much."

I say nothing, clamping my tongue between my teeth as I do my job, praying that she won't deduct her troubles with the faucet from any staff tips.

When I finish, I offer a more than generous compensation to smooth over this minor problem.

"I'd love it if you'd accept a free month's worth of yoga classes. We've just contracted the use of the ballroom twice a week with a very highly rated yogi—"

She interrupts me. "Oh, bless your heart. Do I look like these old bones will be doing headstands anytime soon?"

Mrs. Maxwell is only 50. Five years older than I am. And for the first time ever, I actually feel a little bit sorry for this wealthy woman. Fifty is far too young to call it quits, all other hindrances aside. Age is just a number; I've always believed that.

"You never know what you can do until you try. But if you change your mind, just let me know. In the meantime, let me comp your dinner tonight for your troubles."

She nods. "Free dinner with your chef? Hell, darlin', I might break something on purpose if that's on offer."

I say goodbye to Mrs. Maxwell and then sprint to the supply closet with one word in my mind. Rosie. I need to speak to Rosie as soon as possible--and before I get called to fix, change, or answer questions about one more thing.

This is where I like to hide when I need a second, and all the guest rooms are occupied.

Amid the scent of lavender linen spray and freshly laundered towels, I dial up my best friend.

"Hey babe," she says, gasping.

"Why are you out of breath?" I ask.

"It's tapering week, just finished 10K."

I shake my head at my triathlete friend. She's won the gold medal in her age category for four years running, and this year she wants the whole enchilada.

"If 10K is tapering off, I don't want to know what you do when pushing yourself," I reply.

She laughs hoarsely. "I told you I would train you for free!"

"Your yoga classes, I can handle."

She squeals in excitement. "I'm looking forward to getting started!"

I can hear her slosh water all over her face and down her throat as she catches her breath.

"I offered free classes to Eileen Maxwell, but she turned them down."

Rosie gasps. "Oh my god, you evil bitch!"

The two of us laugh, and I thank god for my friend who lets me rant about my most demanding guests. She knows all about that woman.

"I'm making a shopping list for the classes, and I'm setting aside space in the storage closet by the ballroom. How many yoga mats do you think you'll want in case of walk-ins?"

Rosie hums and thinks it over.

As we finalize the details for everything she'll need, my spirit rises while thinking about the possibility of drawing in a new batch of customers to the inn with this class. The inn does well, but the restaurant is only open on weekends during the off-season due to the sparse number of guests. I'd love it to be open Wednesday through Sunday again, and I've coordinated with the kitchen staff to offer hand-crafted green juice following yoga classes with that in mind.

I tell Rosie about this idea, and she shouts in her delight. I forget how loud she gets when she's high from running sometimes.

"It's good to hear your voice," I tell her. "Good luck this weekend! I wish I could be there."

Rosie snorts. "You work too much. If you take time off, I want you out doing something fun for yourself. Not watching me suffer."

I roll my eyes. But then, that moment earlier, in Caleb's room. He was looking at my collarbones like he might be thinking about sucking the meat right off of them.

Maybe, possibly, I might let someone like him do that.

After I hang up the phone with Rosie and mosey back down to my office, adjacent to the front desk, Caleb's extension rings again.

Heat courses through my veins in annoyance. What does he want now?

Chapter Three

Caleb

Naomi looks slightly less than happy to see me as she did when she came to fix the headboard.

But when one finds his muse, one must memorize every facet of said muse. Even the times when her forehead has the slightest crinkle of annoyance.

"You said there's a problem on the balcony. Are you alright? Did you hurt yourself?"

I flash my most charming crooked grin and reply, "Aw, that's so sweet of you to be worried about me. No, I didn't fall. Yet."

The face that looks back at me is not the face of a woman quickly taken in by charm. Her mouth forms a flat line. "I ask because if you did fall, we need to document this interaction in case you decide to hire a personal injury lawyer." Naomi's green eyes scan me from head to toe, and I detect the slightest pauses at my mouth, my chest, below my belt. My dick twitches at the idea that she might be sizing it up, noticing the outline in my perhaps-too-tight jeans.

"It's the moss."

Her eyes snap to mine, and she cocks her head. "The what?"

I point to the steel floor of the balcony.

"Do you see all that moss?"

We step onto the balcony together, me motioning for her to go first through the narrow windowed door. As she passes by me, her hip brushes against my pelvis. I did not position myself this way on purpose, and the unintentional contact is like plugging in a 1000-volt battery. It's barely a nudge, barely a swipe. It means nothing, but there's no talking sense into my cock. It wants her. I want her. The sooner, the better.

How is it I'm hard as stone after…what I just did less than an hour ago?

Oblivious to my internal torment, Naomi steps onto the balcony and looks down. I stand behind her, perhaps too close, because there's nowhere to stand unless I remove my easel. When she squats to examine the floor, her shirt hikes up. The tattoo above her lower left cheek is of a large, intricate hibiscus flower. Deep, warm pink, with petals spread so wide it's obscene--if one knows anything about plant biology. Flower sex is a thing, and once you know that, you can't unsee what's happening in a lot of well-loved art with plant subjects.

The urge to drag the side of my thumb over that tattoo, memorize it, while rooting my cock between those sweet cheeks from behind…holy shit. My insides are screaming.

I need to capture that color of the hibiscus. The need overwhelms me. Reaching for my brush, I dip my brush into the peach, then the brown, then the red, madly mixing it together to achieve the color of that flower. I've painted a dozen flower still lifes in my day, and none of them inspired me; this one, on her, makes me feel things. Every plane of her middle and every arc of her limbs make me want to paint.

The color…it's not quite right. To say nothing of her skin. I wouldn't know where to begin. She's fair but not alabaster. Peachy, but in shadow, it's got an orange tint. It's going to drive me crazy.

She's caught me staring like a lunatic again. Remaining in a squat, she says in her thick drawl, "This is a north-facing room, so you're going to see some moss," she says. "I'm sure the railing will remain in place and prevent you from tumbling to your demise, however."

Oh my god. I love her.

"Right. The railing."

Naomi stands, and I'm again achingly aware of how close she is in this narrow space. I inhale two full lungs of air, noticing her honeysuckle scent. Honeysuckle and biscuits and sweet tea. I could get drunk on that essence. I bite my lip as I stare, my mind imagining that sweetness between her legs, her honey dripping down my tongue.

"Slippery." I can't help it; I lick my lips and swallow the saliva because I am on the verge of visibly drooling being this close to my muse.

I'm not talking about the moss beneath my feet anymore. Her dilating pupils tell me she knows that. Her eyes dart to my mouth, and her lips part.

She arches an eyebrow. "I'll send someone up with a nonskid mat for you." Officious? Yes, but she also sounded…a bit breathier than before.

"That's exactly what I need. Thank you," I say, smiling down at her.

Naomi turns and slips back into the room, and I stand there, watching her walk away.

"Wait," I say.

She turns. "Something else?" Not precisely impatient, but eager to get on with her day.

"I wonder if you might be interested in sitting for me. For a portrait."

Her lips part in surprise at the question. Those lips are the same color as that hibiscus on her tush. I am as sure of that as I am of my own name.

Naomi closes her mouth, then. With a small smile, she answers, "No."

I smile back, undaunted.

I don't take my eyes off her until she's out of my room again.

Dinner is still three hours away.

What havoc can I wreak next, I wonder?

Chapter Four

Naomi

CALEB CALLS me up to his room twice more this afternoon.

Once, to remind me about the safety mat I promised to have delivered for his balcony so that one's on me.

The next call, which came right between checking in more guests, was complaining about a draft coming through the bathroom window. Gritting my teeth, I'd covered the corners with weatherstripping because that is what I do for guests. Granted, I've never had anyone complain about drafty windows. Sure, they are drafty. But people, in general, understand about these old wood windows and single pane glass.

When I'd finished with the weatherstripping, I'd turned around to find him sketching on a pad in the bathroom doorway.

I was ready to clock him, thinking he was sketching me when my back was turned. That's all I need; my ass turning up on a canvas at a gallery somewhere. But when he'd turned the pad around to show me, it was nothing but a rough charcoal still life of the tray of homemade soaps and essential oils that I keep stocked on the back of the toilet.

I've spent the last fifteen minutes wondering why I was slightly disappointed that he wasn't sketching me. Distractedly, I check in more and more guests as dinner time approaches.

By the time Caleb calls down to the front desk for the fifth time today, I'm about ready to ask him to leave.

I march up to his room, prepared with the entire speech.

"Caleb," I'll say. "Perhaps historic inns are not for you. You may be happier with the Hilton in Gold Hill."

But when he opens his door, he looks…impatient? Frustrated?

Noticing the tick of his jaw, I think, *you and me both, sweetie.*

"What is it this time? The ghost dog of room 2A humping your leg?" I say without thinking.

I thought this might get a laugh, but I get nothing, just a flash of his brown eyes as he turns on his heel and stalks to the center of the room.

I stare at him as he points to the ceiling fan.

Crossing my arms in front of my chest, I tell this irksome fellow that the instructions for the ceiling fan are in the binder on the desk.

"No," he says. "There's a bulb out."

I look up to where he points, and I see that he's correct; only three of the four bulbs appear to be in working order. This might be the only legitimate complaint this fool has had all afternoon.

"Be right back," I say. "I have to fetch the ladder."

He offers to carry it for me. "Sorry, I should have told you what I was calling about. Let me help you."

"No worries," I say tightly, already stalking down the hall to the supply closet. He's next to me, keeping pace with my steps and not letting up. He smells like paint and musky maleness that I do not hate, even though he irks me.

Inside the supply closet, he takes the stepladder out of my hands.

"I can't let you carry that," I say.

"It weighs more than you do."

This fact means nothing to me. "So? This is my job. Give me the ladder."

"Will you sit for a portrait?"

"Mr. Baxter."

"Please call me Caleb."

"Fine. Caleb. I'm swamped, and even if I wanted to sit for a portrait, I couldn't." I gently push past him, eager to get us out of the supply closet.

I see the smirk as he watches me, and all of me would love nothing more than to smother that smartass look off his face. Smother him with what? Throw pillows? My pussy? Why not both?

"You should really hire another handyman," he remarks once we're back in his room. I make a point to leave the door ajar.

I set up the stepladder and climb up to the top step to reach the ceiling fan. "For someone who wants to paint me, you sure seem to want to get rid of me."

"I think you just need to be less busy. I've painted tidal waves that were easier to nail than you."

Rearing back with one hand on the dead lightbulb, I reply, "Excuse me?"

Heat blooms in his sweet young cheeks, and he looks

like he wishes the earth would open up and swallow him whole.

Paint, musk, and the clean scent in this room create a heady combination. I wouldn't say it's making me swoon, but it's reminding me of how long it's been since I tussled in fresh sheets with anyone. Something in my face gives it away that I'm now thinking about sex, because Caleb stammers for the first time in the five hours I've known the man.

"I mean…oh god, I meant nail you down. For a sitting. Wow, that does not sound better than the first thing I said, does it?"

Despite sucking both of my lips into my mouth to keep from laughing, I can't deny the feeling that pricks at me.

How would he nail me, exactly? Feverishly, with me bent over the antique chaise, my fingernails denting the tufted cushions, my voice rasping out a shocked orgasm? Or would he go slowly, leaving no spot of me untouched, untasted, edging me until I cried out his name with tears streaming down my face and my pussy quivering and spent? My gaze rakes over that broad chest, assessing the strength of those arms, those thighs. My insides are melting again at the very idea of his scruffy chin scraping inside my thigh.

Too bad there's no way to know if he has the stamina of a 45-year-old woman. Women of a certain age are a fine and well-crafted wine with many notes to savor. Not to mention a long finish.

My eyes glance at the clock on the nightstand. We have an hour before dinner. Plenty of time to take the boy for a test drive.

No, no, Naomi. Sleeping with the guests? That's a bad look. What would Mrs. Maxwell think if she knew I was contemplating bedding this man I barely know, just down the hall? Indeed, she'd be scandalized.

Suddenly, I remember what I'm doing here. Simply changing a lightbulb. I should be finished and back at the front desk already.

I tear my eyes away from him and get to work.

"That's weird," I say, noticing how the bulb pulls out too quickly. "Hang on a second."

Caleb asks, "What is it?"

There's an off chance that someone might have…but that would be nuts, right? Then again, this is Caleb we're talking about. I twist the light bulb to the right, and it screws in and lights up, bright as day.

I turn toward him, where he is perched on the edge of the bed, sketching away.

"Caleb."

He looks up, his tongue poking out the side of his mouth in concentration. "Uh-huh?"

"Caleb, this light bulb had simply been unscrewed."

He mumbles as he sketches away. From this vantage point atop the stepladder, I can see everything he's drawing. Some kind of flower in a bowl. "That's crazy," he mumbles. "Who does that?"

I sit down on the top step, willing him to look up from the sketch as I tell him, "I once had a sister-in-law who would unscrew lightbulbs until she absolutely needed electricity rather than switch the lights off. I couldn't figure it out. I didn't ask her about it, though, because I thought maybe that was some leftover trauma or something, and I didn't want to embarrass her. I learned never to comment on someone's quirks as a child. My grandpa, whose family nearly starved during the Great Depression, would not let a single food scrap go into the trash. We kids learned not to comment on it. So, I never said anything to my sister-in-law about her weird light bulb habit. Then one day, after my brother divorced her, he told me she did that to keep the government from listening to their conversations. So let me ask you this, Caleb, why would you partially unscrew that bulb? Did you forget your tinfoil hat?"

Nothing of what I said seems to have registered. He is wholly devoted to his sketch pad. "Wow," he mumbles. "You don't say."

It's then that I notice what he's sketching. It's not a flower in a bowl. He is drawing a hibiscus. My hibiscus. The one that's on my ass. And that bowl is not a bowl. Those curves are butt cheeks. My butt cheeks.

I have half a mind to unscrew all the lightbulbs and smash them against his head. But I don't do that. I simply watch him sketch.

I go still as his long fingers drag the charcoal pencil in swirls and arcs on the page. I notice the texture of the paper as the meat of his hand slides over it. I hear the scraping of the tip. The rubbing of the side of it with the shading in that spot right under my cheek.

I'll grant that he peeked at my tattoo once or twice today. But how the hell does he know what my backside looks like? He doesn't.

And yet, he's doing alright.

And then, the side of his thumb slides across the picture to the shadowy area at the juncture of my thighs. I press my legs together, and my breath catches in my throat. The edge of that angled thumb rubs back and forth in that spot, smoothing and blending the charcoal. He erases, fills back in, and repeats. The swiping of that thumb creates a three-dimensional curve, giving the impression of light shining from a window somewhere on a pretty little rump.

My nipples tighten, my sex clamps down as Caleb's thumb smooths over that curve, then he brings that thumb up to his mouth. His brows come together as one while the smudged end of this thumb presses against his lips.

I finally find the words. "Sir…I told you no. Who the fuck do you think you are?"

His eyes snap up to me, with an intense expression, as if I made him lose his train of thought, and he's deeply unhappy about it.

"I think I'm the guy who's no longer asking permission, other than do you want to fuck?"

I take zero seconds to think about it. A simple "Yeah" slips out.

The sketch pad falls to the floor with a flop, and his pencil clatters against the hardwood. Big arms jerk me from the stepladder, and the next thing I know, I am bent over the chaise, just like the scene I had pictured in my head.

Unbuttoning my jeans, I start to work the waistband down, but Caleb pushes my hands away. I'm not moving fast enough. The knowledge of that makes my body turn to liquid. With a grunt, he shoves down my jeans along with my undies.

I'll never forget the sound of his metal belt buckle and zipper. I quiver, waiting for that contact.

A gasp escapes when I feel those paint-and-charcoal smudged hands spread my cheeks, and a knee knocks my legs apart. The next thing that happens pulls all the blood from my brain and pools it right to the juncture of my thighs: something long and rigid plunging in between my folds.

"Oh my god, Naomi. You've been thinking dirty thoughts, haven't you? How else did you get so wet?"

I push back, lubing him up, letting him capture all of my essence and coating every inch of that hard length. "No more than you have," I retort, glancing back at him.

That wild look in Caleb's eyes is still there, but his lip curls in mischief now.

The wet sounds as he coats himself with me are explosive.

But that's nothing compared to the multiple sensations of feeling him sink that girth into me, his arm caged around my front, his charcoal-smudged fingers toying with the tiny, aching bundle of nerves, and my muscles tightening around that delightfully twitchy young cock.

When I push back again, I slowly adapt my muscles to his fullness, stretching me out. He barely waits for my muscles to adjust to his size when he pulls out and thrusts back in, fully seating himself to the hilt. The sensation takes my breath away, and I moan.

"Good?"

"Uh-huh," I rasp, pushing back, trying to take more, but I already have all of him.

"I knew I was gonna be fucking you as soon as I laid eyes on you, Naomi."

There's something sweet in the way he says my name, and it pulls at a tiny thread of sentimentalism that I didn't know existed within me.

Before I can let that thought get to me, he pulls out and slams back in. And again. And again, until our bodies build a wild, frantic rhythm.

Soon, the thick cock and the fingers on my clit nearly have my body seizing from pleasure. My orgasm washes over me, and I rasp out the name of every deity I've ever heard of.

Caleb uses my leg to flip me over to my back, never even pulling out of me a single inch. He plants my thighs around his waist and moves me to the chaise cushion, gently setting me down on my back while kneeling in front of me.

A rough hand jerks up the hem of my shirt and tugs down the bra. My mind slithers into renewed pleasure at the cupping of my breast, his filthy fingers smudging my nipples. A groan from him has me gripping down harder, so I can hear that sound again, but louder. His mouth covers my nipple, warming it with his teasing tongue. The scrape of teeth on it makes me hum, and I dig my nails into his back.

"These nipples," he grits out, "...same color as your lips. Your tattoo. You drive me fucking insane. God, you're so fucking perfect. Where the fuck did you come from?"

I'm still writhing out my orgasm, but I drag my thighs up higher around his torso and demand more. "Still raring to go, that's what I like," he says with a self-satisfied smirk as he again pushes in to the hilt and pulls out again.

Even in the split-second he's out, I feel the empty space.

Mrs. Maxwell's voice echoes in the hallway as people stroll by on their way to dinner, as Caleb and I grind and grunt against each other. It occurs to me the door is still ajar.

Grunting and writhing, our bodies still claiming each other like two simple-minded mammals in a pasture, neither of us seem to care. If anything, there's an unspoken challenge between us. His eyes fix on mine with wild alertness, expecting me to push him away at any second. Breathless, his lips are parted and curved in a half-smile as his cock drives in and out of me with abandon.

That's when I arc up off the chaise, and he roots in harder, fiercer, again and again, leaning down to cover me with that broad chest and stealing a fiery, licking kiss from my mouth. For a moment, we seem to share breath.

He squeezes my ass cheek when he comes inside me, so hard and fierce that his face freezes. The vein on his forehead matches the pulsing of his cum. He curses through gritted teeth, and it's that release of sheer tension, knowing that for hours, he's been thinking of doing nothing but this, that sends me barreling through a second climax.

"Holy shit, Caleb!"

"That's my girl."

Nobody, nobody calls me that. I have gleefully reduced men to quivering single-celled organisms for calling me girl, sweetie, honey.

So why do I let it slide with him? More to the point, why does it make me squirt on top of my second orgasm?

We slow but do not let go of each other as we finish. Caleb collapses on top of me, his face nestling between my breasts, with a heavy, hoarse declaration: "What have you done to me, Peaches? What have you done?"

His breath against my breast is hot, but it wafts across my still-hard nipple. He hums devilishly when he sees it and moves over me to take that nipple into his mouth. Again.

Damn, I should be pushing him off right now, but I don't want to. That touch, his licking, sucking, and nibbling, is perfect.

Combined with his caresses to these melons, he soon has me purring like a kitten and rubbing my inner thighs up his damp torso again.

Wickedly, he chuckles against my breast, and the sound vibrates through me.

As if he hardly noticed how hard I came already—twice—Caleb heaves himself off of me, knees back onto the floor, and positions me so my hips are held tight in place with his hands. It seems I weigh next to nothing for him as he arches my limp pelvis upward, spreads my lips with two thumbs, and places a damp kiss directly on my button.

I don't think I can take anymore, but holy hell, he gives it anyway. Soon I'm squirming, my body jerking, my arousal spiking with every swipe and suckle against that particular spot. Without thinking, I fist his hair, grinding against him.

His laughter against my taut center pushes me through to the loudest, most frenzied orgasm I've ever felt.

"Say my name this time when you come." The commanding tone makes the two sides of my brain implode. I fucking hate bossy people, but I also love it. Fuck him; he's rearranged everything.

I explode at his cockiness, but how could I deny him that one tiny thing after what he just did to me?

"Caleb," I rasp, my body shuddering, sweat dripping from my thighs.

"My girl."

Thank god, he lets me catch my breath before kissing me again.

I move to push him off me when I catch sight of the clock on the nightstand. I'm officially late for dinner now.

"Hang on. I'm not quite finished with you yet," he says roughly, turning me over on my stomach again.

He couldn't possibly extract anything else from me. Three orgasms in 20 minutes must be a record.

Is he going to go in the back door? At six p.m. on a Friday? Would I let him? Oh, hell yeah. I can be super late for dinner for once. Let the hostess schmooze the guests for once.

But it's not the contact I expect, not at first. Only a slow, warm scrape of callouses over my left lower back. When I glance over my shoulder, I see Caleb tracing his fingers reverently over my hibiscus tattoo, my full ass bare to him.

Unexpectedly, he leans forward and presses a kiss

against the design, closing his eyes as if in worship. This small gesture does something to me. It pulls on the last thread of my assumptions about this beautiful young artist.

At that moment, I wonder if this is more to him than just a quick fuck to get each other out of our systems.

Either way, I'm extremely late for dinner.

Chapter Five

Caleb

"Was that the meal to end all meals, or what?"

Now, I know Naomi is not asking about the meal I just made of her body, all over the chaise lounge in my room. That was the best twenty minutes of my entire existence.

No, she's talking about the steak I just demolished with a side of cheesy smashed potatoes. She slides a plate with a slice of butterscotch pie in front of me.

"It was," I tell her, raking my eyes across her breasts. "And I plan on devouring you again later."

Her cheeks heat.

"Caleb," she murmurs, leaning in closer to admonish me. "This is a family establishment, and people can hear you."

I glance around the room and shoot back. "Don't see any children around. Unless you mean me. Obviously, I already know about the birds and the bees. Got an A in health class. It was only a few years ago, so as you can tell, it's fresh in my memory."

She shakes her head, but I see how her gaze travels over my body. I note the rise and fall of her chest as she takes a deep breath.

"I better get back to work," she says. "We're short a server."

As she turns to walk away, I murmur, "Make it a quick shift. I got more issues for you to address with my room later."

Her footsteps pause. I could be seeing things, but I detect a slight shiver in her frame at my words.

If I knew I would be watching half a dozen people pawing all over my female, I would have taken my dessert in my room. As it is, this is torture. Is it any surprise that everyone loves her and wants to be closer to her?

My brain knows that schmoozing with guests is part of Naomi's job. My ass-backward male ego wants to punch every man's lights out who puts his hand on her.

I watch her float through the room from my corner table, delivering food and clearing dishes. Pouring wine and chatting with guests. Many of them seem to know her. Many of them older, distinguished men her age with silver hair. The kind of rich men that likely have things called tax shelters and other things I can't fathom. I do all right. I have enough to live simply.

On the one hand, I could sit here and wonder what I think I'm doing, aiming at a woman so far out of my league. On the other hand, good for me. Look at her. She's mine. I can still smell her on me. This is the way I prefer to look at it.

She's mine and if I have to never check out of this inn so I can stay close to her forever, then so be it.

"Was that the best meal of your life or wasn't it?" She

asks this of one solo gentleman in a three-piece suit, who flashes a row of sparkling white teeth at her.

So, that's her line, is it? I guess I can get past it.

What I can't get past is that stuffed suit she's talking to. Rage fills me as he reaches for her hand, pulls her close, and closes his second hand over hers. "Everything was fantastic, including the service." He gestures to the chair next to his at his table. "Sit and have a drink with me, won't you? It's been too long."

Who the fuck is that, and what does he think he's doing with his hands on her?

Before I can stop myself, I'm on my feet. Without a word, I sidle up to the table where Naomi stands and slip my arm around her waist.

Naomi's gaze snaps to mine in surprise.

"Caleb!" There's a flash of something fearful in her eyes, like I might do something unprofessional to her in front of the other guests. Honestly, I would not put it past me. I'm so beside myself with needing to claim her for myself that I would have zero problems asking her for a ride against the wall right here in the dining room. I'd love to see that mask of professionalism gone and replaced with that wild, scratching, clawing kitty that I just fucked in my room twenty minutes ago.

With a slightly too proud look on my face, I gaze down at the silver-haired man at the table, who looks equally surprised. "Naomi, you didn't tell me your son was visiting from out of town."

There is no way I'm young enough to be her son. Where does this guy get off?

Naomi takes it all in stride. "No, Everette. Jason's only 19, and he lives in Colorado with his dad in the summers. This is Caleb. He's...he's a friend. An artist! A visiting artist friend. Caleb, this is Everette Foster. He's pretty much the whole reason this building is still standing."

Everette sees me glaring at the way he is clasping her hand and, with a raised eyebrow, lets go of her. He rests a hand on his sternum, and his expression is all phony humility. "I wouldn't go that far," he says.

Naomi protests. "I never would have gotten that small business loan to fix the place up if it weren't for you," she replies.

My hand at her waist drifts lower until I grip her hip, my fingers anchoring me to her body. I would love it if Naomi could stop paying compliments to this man who obviously (to me, anyway) has the hots for her.

She feels my fingers gently digging in. I know this because I see the way her tiny earlobes turn pink. I see the flare in her nostrils. She's annoyed with me…but not that annoyed. Good. I can't wait to show her what it does to me to see other men undress her with their eyes.

Everette forces me to look away from Naomi with a clearing of his throat. "Well, I didn't become bank president in Gold Hill by turning away the deserving small businesswomen. Fate needed some sprucing up." Then he changes his tone ever so slightly as he turns his attention to me. "Artist, you say? What kind of artist?"

I keep my eyes trained on my muse. Her neck. Her ear, her halo of blonde-turning-white hair. The spark in her eyes as she tries to tell me to be normal with this Very Important Man. I answer, "Oil on canvas, mostly. Some watercolor. And also murals."

Everette remarks. "Where might I have seen your work?"

Mentioning the bridge I'd just completed for a small city in southern Ohio, he makes a noise of acknowledgment. "Yes, I think I've seen that while maneuvering in bumper-to-bumper traffic on my way to Dayton for a bank acquisition last month. Well, my driver was doing the maneuvering, not me. I was on the phone, of course. The only way to stay on top of all the work is to work during the commute. But that's great for you. Your parents must be proud that you're putting your art degree to good use. Where did you say you went to school?"

I feel Naomi stiffen next to me. Everette has said too much now, and she can finally see him for what he is. A condescending prick. "I didn't go to art school. And my parents are dead."

Naomi seems to melt into me when I say this. Her expression is full of sympathy. But that's the last thing I want from her.

"My daughter's in art school," Everette mutters out of the side of his mouth, but neither Naomi nor I are paying him any attention. She's trying to read my face, trying to apologize with her eyes for this man bringing up the subject of my dead parents. "I told her to go into graphic design; that's at least an employable skill."

I wish this man would shut up. I think I'll have to make that happen on my own. "Tell your daughter not to set her hopes on graphic design. Tell her to pursue what makes her happy."

I know what makes me happy. One person makes me happy, and she's standing right here, looking deeply uncomfortable.

Naomi pulls away from me then and begins to clear Everette's dishes. "Can we bring you any dessert?"

"Just the check," he replies, eyeing me as I take everything from Naomi's hands and haul the tray of dirty dishes to the kitchen.

It all goes according to plan, as she's now following me into the kitchen.

Chapter Six

Naomi

I HISS as I follow Caleb into the kitchen, his arms laden with dirty dishes that I'm meant to be carrying.

"What are you doing? You are a guest, Mr. Baxter!"

"Mister Baxter," he says once we are through the swinging doors. "That's cute. Make sure you call me that later."

I shouldn't be surprised at how brazen he's being, even in front of my kitchen staff. The man rutted me with his room door open. And I went along with it.

A shiver runs through me. And I'd do it again, I think to myself. What's wrong with me? This is not who I am.

Or is it?

"Caleb, please have a seat and finish your dessert," I implore him.

"Oh, I plan to finish my dessert," he says, unloading his dishes on the cart next to the commercial dishwasher. Steam pours from the unit as a fresh batch of clean dishes comes out on the conveyor belt. I start to back away, worried about the effect of this steam on my silk blouse, but Caleb isn't having it. Instead, his large fist clutches my wrist.

What a way for a man to grab a woman. And yet. I don't object as he hauls me through the kitchen's rear door, past the composting and recycling bins.

"Where are you taking me? I have work to do."

He says nothing but seems to be stalking, hunting for something, growing increasingly frustrated.

His arms cage me against the wood fence separating the truck delivery driveway from the back gardens.

The fire in his eyes unsettles me but doesn't scare me; I've seen it before, not that long ago, in his room.

Caleb towers over me, and I can smell his paint cleaner and whiskey.

"Caleb," I stammer.

He does something wholly unexpected then by nuzzling my neck with his nose. "I missed you." And here I'd thought I was about to get a hickey.

I huff out a dry laugh. "I'm in the middle of dinner."

Against my neck, he murmurs, "Hire more people."

"I have enough. People have lives, kids get sick, people are humans who need days off, and I can't afford to hire a legion of workers."

"I don't want to talk about staffing anymore," he says with a low, lethal rasp. I'm about to ask him what he means when his hand scrapes up the hem of my skirt and cups a handful of my ass cheek.

I gasp, but I don't push him away. Why don't I instantly push him away? Because I'm wet, and I want him to know. I want him to find it.

"Please just say what you have to say so I can get back to work; this is insane." My words are insistent, but my insides are jelly. Never in my life has a man demanded so much attention so soon after sex. No one has ever been this ready to go again so quickly.

"I don't like that guy," he finally rasps, his eyes on mine.

My eyes narrow. "What guy?"

Caleb mimics Everette's odd way of laughing, and I know.

"Oh my god. You're jealous," I point out.

Caleb's hot whiskey mouth is on mine, and his tongue is down my throat. Could there be any louder confirmation of jealousy than that? I drink in his whiskey tongue and let him slam my hips against his. I grind against that length, and both of us know how good it would feel right now, both of us wanting that feeling again.

I moan into his mouth, and the sound he gives me back is pornographic.

He pulls back from the kiss, and his hand moves to my front, his fingers skating over my panties.

"Listen," he orders, tugging the fabric crotch to the side, devastating me with the touch of his fingers between my folds. "I don't like that guy. I don't like the way he talks to you."

The pads of Caleb's fingers drag through my wetness, and the sensation threatens to pull a kittenish mewl out of me. "I don't like the way he looks at you," he adds, his jaw ticking, his digit sinking into my cunt and stretching me. "And I definitely do not like the way he touches you."

He sinks in a second finger, and the two of those wicked digits work me over, in and out. My mouth goes dry, and I'm helpless. I feel like I'm drugged. How else do I explain letting a man fifteen years my junior finger bang me out back of my own inn?

Like a man who knows what he's doing, Caleb's fingers

inside me make a "come hither" motion, and I'm done for. Unlike the world disappearing before when he'd fucked me in his room, at this moment, I'm hyper-aware of everything. The smell of the wood pressing against my sweaty back. The taste of his mouth on my lips. The evening sun smears the sky behind his head with a pink and orange halo, my favorite color. Yes, his fingers moving inside me, hurtling me closer to orgasm, but also noticing how quickly those fingers get to the point. How he knows my body so well in such a short amount of time. And the birds. I hear the hummingbirds buzzing in the feeders just on the other side of this wall. And I remember how those hummingbird feeders hang just outside the windows of the main dining room, where Everette is sitting, undoubtedly bewildered by a fellow guest having cleared his table.

A part of me, the nurturing aspect, wants to reassure Caleb he has nothing to worry about. Everette is married and would never really try anything. Sure he's a flirt and a bit clueless about the stuff that comes out of his mouth, but he doesn't see me that way. Does he?

And yet…some deep, dark, wicked part of me likes that Caleb is jealous. No one has ever taken me out back for a talking-to. No one would dare.

Despite being utterly overwhelmed by his fingers inside me, his breath wafting over my face, I manage a wry smile.

"But I have to be nice to my guests. I have to shake their hands. Don't be unreasonable, Caleb."

The skin is tight around his jaw. Not a single flaw on that beautiful young face. So youthful, so full of life, and the overwhelming need to live it.

His fingers work me over so insistently that I forget everything. His words skate over the skin of my collarbone, and his voice drops an octave. "Don't think I can't tell, sweetheart. You're so fucking wet. You love it that I'm out of my mind right now. Tell me how many guys like that would take you like this."

"Caleb."

He seethes while his thumb paints circles around my clit, his first two fingers already destroying my pussy. "How many?" Caleb grits out. The wet noises my body makes. My god, if someone sees us…

If someone sees us, who cares? I own the joint. People love to gossip. Give them something to talk about.

"None. Nobody would, and nobody could," I breathe.

He kisses me again, playfully, teasing my lips with his tongue while his thumb swipes my sensitive clit, and again those fingers inside sweep forward. "You know that's fuckin' right," he breathes.

And then my mouth slackens, and my release barrels through me like a freight train.

"And I'll tell you another thing," he rasps, pebbling my face, neck, and collarbone with kisses as I ride out my release against his devastating hand. "I ain't checking out of here anytime soon."

This man is not a 30-year-old kid. This man is a freak who can keep up with my needs. No, he roots out my innermost needs and shows them to me. And then fills them.

I don't know how much more I can take of this and run this inn simultaneously.

But he's right about one thing. I'm going to need to hire help.

Chapter Seven

Caleb

This is the most uncomplicated phone call I've ever made about a life-changing decision.

"Hey, Jake. It's me."

A snort followed by the words, "You're not coming home for the Fourth, are you?"

My brother already knows I'm about to drop a bomb. I'm a son of a bitch and an artist who's bound to bounce at any minute. In the years we've lived together, I've spent maybe 30 days at our two-flat in Chicago. I usually try to make it home for the fireworks in July.

"How'd you know?"

"I can hear it in your voice. What is it this time? Another mural in Venice Beach that pays pennies?"

I bark out a laugh and tell him, "Nah. Better than that. I found my muse."

A silence follows.

"So, what's that mean? No more public murals? No

more teaching gigs? You're finally gonna paint what you want?"

That's the least of it.

"Better. I'm going to be an artist in residence at this hotel I'm staying at."

"Who is she?"

"You're not going to believe this, but she's the owner."

Jake makes a humming noise like he's considering something. "You're not thinking of sleeping on her couch until you make your next move?"

"Jake," I protest. "You have me confused for someone else. When have I ever done that?"

I can practically hear him rubbing the scruff of his chin. "I dunno. I bet your exes would be able to answer that."

The truth is, I used to sleep on one or two exes' sofas after our parents kicked me out. But that was when I was 18 and 19.

"I'd like to think I have grown a little since then, Jake."

"Doubt it. Hey, what is that noise? Are you in a jacuzzi?"

I turn off the water of Naomi's deep soak tub and begin to light the candles that I ran out and bought for tonight, among other things. "No," I tell him. "I'm running a bath for her. She'll be tired when she's done with work tonight, so I'm gonna try to do something nice. I've been kind of a demanding asshole."

Jake sounds taken aback when I say this. "Really? Wow. Okay. Maybe you have changed."

I'm not sure I know what he means. I've always simply been me.

"Sorry if this leaves you in the lurch, brother."

He scoffs. "Are you kidding? I was giving you a

discount. I've got a waiting list of potential renters, so think nothing of it. But I'll miss you."

"I'll book a room for you. You might like it. Who knows, you might find your muse."

"Don't need a muse; I'm a contractor, dumbass."

Ah, my loving brother.

I say goodbye and get back to work.

I have to get everything ready for Naomi.

There's not gonna be a single thing for her to fix tonight. I'm gonna fix her up real good.

Chapter Eight

Naomi

WHEN THE DINNER SHIFT ENDS, my feet are screaming, my joints are sore, and I'm covered in a sheen of perspiration.

Running an inn is hard, and filling in when I'm short-staffed is getting more and more taxing on my body.

Middle age. In my case, it means an unquenchable libido and yet a complete lack of energy after six p.m. Thanks, I hate it.

The orgasms are pretty fucking great, though. Probably because I'm no longer worried about getting pregnant.

Just as I'm stiffly stumbling into my apartment that adjoins my office, Rosie calls.

"Babe, shouldn't you be resting up for the big event tomorrow?" I ask her, kicking off my shoes and blowing out a breath of relief.

"I'm drunk, and I'm calling you, so I don't post something stupid on my ex's page," Rosie replies.

"Rosie. Stop what you're doing right now and drink

some water. Take a Tylenol. Eat some eggs and go to bed. You do not want to run hungover, you lunatic."

She laughs like this is the funniest thing she's ever heard. This is nothing new, by the way. She and her Ironman friends routinely think it's hilarious to get drunk the night before. It makes absolutely no sense to me.

"What are you doing right now?"

I tell her I'm about to shower and go to bed. I am getting ready to pull my shirt off when there's a rustling in the bathroom. So help me, if someone has wandered in here looking for me to do more work…

"Hang on, babe, I gotta get my frying pan to clock someone."

I open the bathroom to find Caleb standing there with a lit candle in one hand and a pair of soft spa slippers in the other.

My first reaction is to curse.

"What the hell are you doing?"

I hear Rosie shout something on the phone. "I'm okay, Rosie. It's just my…uh…my friend. It's a long story."

"Oh no, you don't. Put him on the phone."

"Absolutely not," I say.

With a mischievous smile that threatens to turn my world upside down, Caleb sets the candle on a side table and takes the phone from me.

"I can hear every single word. Hi. This is Caleb; you wanted to talk to me?"

I try to grab the phone from him, but he's much stronger than me. Through the phone, I hear Rosie ask, "Are you a platonic friend or an orgasm friend?"

I slap my hands over my eyes. I cannot believe this is happening.

To my slight disappointment, I hear him say, "Neither."

I slide my hands away from my eyes, and his gaze tells me he's teasing. "I'm her orgasm boyfriend."

Rosie shrieks and Caleb pulls the phone away lest she blow out one of his eardrums.

"Excuse me?" I ask, but only feigning indignation. After that stunt outside the kitchen, the jealousy, the intensity, I know this man is out of his mind. For now. Who knows what will happen when he checks out of the inn next month.

Rosie says something I can't hear. She knows I'm listening.

Caleb lifts an eyebrow and looks at me. "Really," he says. "Sure, tell me."

I don't know what she's telling Caleb, but I'm sure I disapprove of the information she's sharing with him.

With his eyes on me, he listens, running the side of his thumb over his bottom lip. He stares at me with the most wicked grin I've seen on him yet.

"Thanks for that information, Rosie. You've been a huge asset. I'm looking forward to meeting you…why yes, I'd be very interested in attending your yoga class this weekend. Sounds like I'll need to stay limber, that's for sure."

I can't take it anymore. Holding out my hand, I demand that he give me my phone back.

"Rosie," I start, trailing off when I notice the aroma of citrus and chamomile hit me. Instantly, my muscles begin to relax.

While I continue to chat with Rosie and address the original reason she called—to get her mind off the urge to post on her ex's social media page—I undress and sink into the tub. Caleb is near but doesn't intrude on the conversation or get me to try to hang up the phone. He doesn't demand my attention, not until Rosie and I finish our discussion. I wish her luck tomorrow and hang up.

He takes the phone and sets it on the bathroom counter, then perches on the tub's edge.

I pull him down even with my face. "Thank you," I say, pressing a kiss to his lips. "Unfortunately, you won't be able to stay for too long tonight; I have an early morning with the cleaning crew."

"No, you don't," he says, lifting up one of my feet from the water and massaging my tired ankle. It feels so good I almost don't register what he said. "Um…wait, what? Yes, I do. That wasn't me trying to get rid of you, Caleb."

Confidently, he smiles down at me and massages the other ankle, setting the first one back into the water gently. "I know you're not trying to get rid of me. I've got someone else to help the cleaning crew in the morning."

"Who? If you hired a one-time helper, I have paperwork to fill out…."

Caleb shushes me softly and runs a hand up over my calf. "I need you to be still, and let me take care of you."

Something in his voice compels me to listen. I huff out a laugh, but I'm complying nonetheless. "Nobody tells me what to do. At least a dozen people told me not to buy this place. They said it was a money pit. Which it is. But these last few years have been the happiest of my life. Yes, I'm tired, but I love interacting with people. I love this place. I feel like I've built something that matters. I like making people happy and being a place where people make memories."

Caleb's fingers move up higher along the backs of my calves, kneading the tight muscles and pushing me into a deeper state of relaxation.

"Sit forward," he says. I obey, clasping my arms around my knees and resting my head on my forearm as Caleb gently scrubs my back, neck, and shoulders with the sudsy loofah. I let out a long, satisfied sigh.

"I could get used to this," I say.

"You will," he replies. "This is my job now."

I snort. "You have a life. And art to…art."

He pauses his rubdown, and I lift my head to see what could be coming next. But he's just staring at me.

"I wasn't joking when I said I wasn't leaving. I'm staying here to take care of you. Do you need someone to do handyman things around the inn? I'll do it. Need a housekeeper? More wait staff? I'm your guy."

"Do you even know how to make a bed? I already know you know how to break them," I tease.

Whatever salts he has put in this bath are working their magic because my tired, stiff joints are feeling much better now. I feel loose enough that I'm not questioning his plans to help me out around the inn tomorrow. Am I really going to let a near-stranger help the housekeepers?

"I know how to make hospital corners. My brother was in the military and whips my ass into shape every time I go home to Chicago."

"Fine," I say, smiling. "But if housekeeping tries to share the tips with you, you need to report that income to the IRS."

"Oh, I think my girlfriend, the former CPA, could probably handle doing my taxes."

"You really know how to crank up a girl's engines, don't you?"

"Let's not forget, I am actually a flakey artist. I can't be good at everything."

A hum escapes me as I luxuriate under his massages. "I don't know. You seem to be good at everything you put your hands on," I say, blinking up at him.

"Whatever you need doing, I'll at least try."

Sitting up, I feel oddly shy at being naked as the bubbles start to dissipate. "You probably don't want to be here for this, but I have to wash my hair and rinse the suds off in the shower."

"Let me," he says, reaching for the shampoo bottle on the shelf next to the tub.

I suppose it won't be the end of the world if I let him wash my hair. How wrong could one person do shampoo?

The next thing I know, the tension in the delicate muscles of my face lets go under the warm water flowing over my head and face. Lovingly, he uses the spray attachment to wet my hair, shielding my eyes from the shampoo and the water. His strong fingers massage the shampoo into my scalp, and I feel my soul settle in for a long night's sleep. Warm water spills over my scalp. I am soothed by the firm movement of his fingers, the scent of the herbal shampoo and the bath salts and the candles. All of it together makes me fall into a trance of complete relaxation. It's like my entire body has unclenched.

Somehow, I drift off to sleep throughout the washing/rinsing/conditioning/rinsing again cycle.

He barely allows the cold air to hit my skin before he has me wrapped up in a soft bath sheet as he blots me dry.

"What next?"

"Hmm?"

His soft chuckle reverberates through my body.

"What else do you do before bed. Do you have like a skin thing?"

A skin regime with night creams and things. That's what he means.

"Yes, over there," I tell him, moving to walk over to my vanity.

He's already helping me by pulling out my little stool for me. Once I'm seated, he asks, "What's first?"

I pause. "Caleb, you're not going to do my night serums."

"Yes, ma'am."

The idea that he wants to do this for me, that he's somehow getting pleasure from pampering me to the point of near ridiculousness, is giving me butterflies. I like this. A lot. I'm an independent woman, but there is something to be said for a man who won't let you lift a finger when you look a little tired.

I insist on removing my own makeup, but he does everything that comes after that. Smoothing the cotton balls of micellar water over my face, applying my toner, dabbing my eye cream with his ring finger—he does all of it.

The feel of his fingers, the look of utter concentration on his face. It's not unlike watching him paint. I love this. So much.

"You have utterly perfect bone structure. Your cheekbones, your chin. My god, woman. The genes are astounding."

I can't fight the blush that heats my cheeks. "If this is a ploy to memorize my face so you can paint me, well, then fine."

Caleb's lips purse in a small smile as he gently massages my night serum over the lines in my forehead. "I memorized your face the second I met you today."

A shiver rolls over me.

He follows up the skin routine by brushing my wet hair, working out all the tangles. Every contact lights up the nerve endings. After letting him massage me, bathe me, shampoo me, I should be touched-out. But every single touch sends a fresh zap of energy into my nerve endings.

I'm loose, warm, and sleepy when he's finished with me.

"My legs still work, you know," I tell him with a smirk when I find myself being swept up from my stool and cradled in his two arms.

"You have to learn to let me do things, or else we'll be having these same conversations every night for the rest of our lives," he says.

The rest of our lives? I do not have the energy to poke holes in that statement. And…do I even want to?

Is he that serious?

I find out just how serious when he makes me his little spoon in the bed. I don't bother pointing out that I skipped the pajamas and went to bed in my satin bathrobe.

I hum softly as I settle into my pillow, noticing how nicely my body fits against his.

"I thought you had plans to devour me," I croak sleepily.

Caleb murmurs against my hair, spreading warmth over my skull. "Sleep first."

He knows. He knows I'm tired but that I'll be down for…whatever he has planned later on.

I stroke the arm that's currently propping my head like a pillow. "How did you get so sweet?"

"I'm only sweet with you," I hear him say.

Chapter Nine

Caleb

I MAY NEVER SLEEP AGAIN as long as I lie next to Naomi. And I plan on being next to Naomi every night for the rest of our lives.

Who needs sleep? I exist only to take care of her, and when I'm not doing that, to paint her. So many ways I want to paint her.

For the moment, I'm happy to lie here and listen to her even breathing. Even if my arm falls asleep.

She begins to mumble in her sleep, and I pet her hair until she settles a few minutes later.

Damn this annoying erection, because I know she feels it when the stirring begins in earnest. The friction of her hips only makes it harder.

I hear her sigh, feel her chest rise and fall where I still have my arm wrapped tight around her. "Good morning," she says.

"It's three a.m.," I inform her.

"Hmm," she says, reaching a hand behind her back and stroking the aching bulge below my navel. "Someone thinks it's time for breakfast," she replies with a sexy laugh.

I should tell her to go back to sleep and not worry about my little problem, but goddamn the way her hand feels. I can only selfishly grunt and push against her. More pressure, more touching, more everything--I need all of it. I tell her this with my body, even if my words admonish her.

"Baby, you need more sleep," I rasp.

"So do you. Whenever I wake up horny at 3 a.m. I reach for my vibrator, but I can't let that go without giving it the attention it needs."

I nip her ear, then slowly lick the spot where my teeth were. "That's hot. Show me."

She giggles. "Show you my vibrator?"

Smoothing her hair away from her ear, I murmur into it. "Show me you, using your vibrator."

The sexy, creaky laugh of hers is sending me.

"Fine," she sighs, still chuckling and reaching for her nightstand drawer. "But I'm not turning on the light. Too bright."

"Fair enough," I say, turning over to light a candle.

I roll away to let her spread out on her back, and already my chest misses her. But what the light reveals next might make me forget the snuggling part.

With her knees bent and her legs spread, her delicate, feminine fingers spread open her folds, wet with her sweetness.

Need floods my veins at the sight of her stickiness, but I will myself to be still. To just watch without touching her. I hear a click, and the ridged phallic end of that toy begins to hum and vibrate. It rolls up and down and throughout her folds, already provoking a delicate hum of pleasure from Naomi's mouth.

She places the butterfly antenna near her clit. Almost instantly, she's coming apart. The sight, and not to mention the sound, might be the most erotic thing I've ever experienced.

It doesn't take long before she's coming apart with a sharp gasp and a sexy, animalistic grunt.

I can't take it anymore. I might actually be drooling all over Naomi's pillows.

But somehow, I manage to snag the toy away to wash it for her in the bathroom.

When I return to the bed, Naomi has switched on the lamp. She's completely naked, having ditched the bathrobe and pulled down the covers for me.

I shake off my pajama bottoms and drawers and slide in next to her, savoring the heat that still pours off of her from that climax I just watched.

I leave no inch of her unkissed, unadored.

I slowly kiss my way down between her legs, hoisting her beautiful thighs up around my shoulders and plummeting my face into her sweetness. The musky, spicy honey overwhelms my senses. I take it all in. I drink all of it, making out with her pussy like it's fucking prom night. The only difference is I have no curfew, and I take all the time I want.

My tongue massages her opening, delving in to claim what belongs to me. I kiss and nuzzle her folds, toying and rubbing until she squirts. The noises she makes make me feel like a champion.

Her fingers thread through my hair, her body demanding a firmer contact. I give it, I give her everything she needs and more. Sucking her clit into my mouth, I nip and play with it until her thighs are trembling.

A big part of me has decided that we're not even close to being done here. To hell with sleep, to hell with a midnight quickie. I don't know if my cock and my ego are one and the same, but they have the same goal: fuck that vibrator. We can make her come harder, louder, and longer than that.

"Hang on, baby girl," I say against her sweetness.

"Caleb," she begs. "Don't stop."

Caging her in under my arms and legs on the mattress, her glassy eyes search me for mercy where there is none.

I sink into her sweetness without breaking eye contact, losing myself in her grip.

"Fuck me, sweetheart. You feel amazing."

Her soft whimpers and hot breath feather over my skin as we began our slow, luxurious fucking.

Soon I realize, as the shine in her eyes squeezes my heart, that this is not fucking. We are actually making love.

With another deep, slow thrust, I can't hold back all the words.

"Naomi."

"Caleb?"

"I love you."

Her eyes widen, and her lips part in surprise.

"Are you surprised? I live my entire life by my gut, and you are it for me, Naomi. I knew as soon as I met you. I love you, and I will always love you."

She bites down on her lip and squeezes her eyes shut. A tear leaks from her eyes.

I slow down to savor the salty taste and kiss away the tear. "Baby, are you okay?"

"I think I love you, too. This is crazy."

"I know, I know."

Scooping her into my arms, I settle her on top of my chest until the tears pass.

Naomi delivers a long, sweet kiss to my lips. Then she sits up and mounts me.

I can do nothing but explode with love at the sight of my Naomi. My woman. My person.

I cup her soft breast in one hand.

A whimper escapes her, and her hand goes downward, but I grasp it with mine.

She gasps. "What are you doing?"

"Sit for me."

Breathily she answers, "What?"

"Pose for me, and I'll finish you."

Her eyes widen when she realizes what I'm doing. I'm refusing to finish her off until she agrees. "Fuck me. You did not just give me an ultimatum."

I give her a sly smile. "Not so much an ultimatum as an offer."

As she moves on me, taking in all of me, milking me until there's nothing left but for me to come so hard.

"I can wait for your answer," I reply. "I'm not going anywhere."

Together we move, neither of us really knowing who is in control. My hands grip her hips like a vise, and she's riding me hard. Together we reach the summit and then plummet off the cliff in our release. The orgasm floods me with so much light I'm blind except for her face.

"Shit. Oh, shit. Peaches."

A wicked smile creeps across her face. "I'll pose for you, Caleb."

"Naked?"

"Don't push it."

Chapter Ten

Naomi

Sleep is overrated. Or maybe my hours count as double when I have a big, meaty mattress of a man to sleep on.

"Someone's got a smile for me this morning."

I snap out of my rosy daydream to come face to face with Everette, who hands me his room key.

His silky voice does nothing for me, but I can see now what Caleb is talking about. The man has a thing for me. How did I not see it before?

It would not be the worst thing in the world. It's flattering. Even as I see him as a friend. But this is more than flattery. My suspicion is confirmed when he hands me the room key, and one thumb brushes across the soft tissue inside my wrist.

"Oh, my goodness," I say with a shy laugh, taking the key and keeping my eyes on the ledger.

"How was your stay, Everett?"

"Lovely as always. I didn't accomplish everything I wanted, but that's business," he says with a wry smile that I catch just as Caleb strolls behind him.

My eyes widen as I see Caleb raise a hand. For a second, I think something terrible is about to happen, but of course, it doesn't. He simply pats him on the back.

"Taking off?"

Everette turns and flashes Caleb a wary smile. Caleb shakes his hand and shows him all his teeth in a smile that might be psychotic. I watch the two men shake hands.

"Yes. And sadly, you'll be off to your next adventure as a transient artist soon. But I'll be just up the road. As I always am, when my little gem of an innkeeper needs me," Everette says.

Finally, I see it. Caleb was right. Everette has been tossing me clues for years that he wants me in his bed, and I've been utterly oblivious. But now that I can see the way he glowers at Caleb, at the way I look at Caleb, I notice everything.

Caleb laughs with an edge of triumph. "Have fun crunching those numbers, big guy. I'll be here when you decide to come back for a visit."

"Oh?" asks Everette.

Caleb nods. "I've accepted the position as artist in residence at the inn. It's an up-and-coming place, and I'd like to stay put for as long as possible."

"I see," Everette replies, looking between Caleb and me.

Finally, he departs with a friendly wave from me. "Say hi to your wife for me."

In a most unprofessional display, Caleb slides behind the front desk, and I wrap my arms around his waist. "What was that about, artist in residence?" I could be annoyed at his presumptuousness, but I like the mental image of Caleb setting up a studio here. I feel a thrill at the idea of going about a day's work, looking out the window and seeing him there, maybe by the lake, painting a canvas.

He sees my smile and kisses me softly three times in a row.

I'm knocked out of this sweet moment with the noise of someone clearing her throat.

Mrs. Maxwell. "Checking out?" I say with a smile.

"Yes," she says, eyeing Caleb suspiciously. "And I've changed my mind. I'd like to purchase a full set of yoga classes."

"Oh?" I'm shocked. "What changed your mind?"

Again, with her eyes casting up and down Caleb, she smirks. Turning back to me, she says, "I've decided. Age is just a number. I think I might like to stay limber. From what I have heard—or overheard—young men can wear a girl out."

When her eyes meet mine, I realize what she's saying. She overheard everything, saw something, or she just knows.

My entire body is aflame under her gaze. I quickly sign her up for classes and hand her her receipt.

Once she's gone, Danny Bryce shows up to talk about redesigning the back garden by the lake. I say goodbye to Caleb, who only agrees to leave me alone with Danny when I promise that Danny is married and his wife would skin me alive if I so much as winked at Danny.

I watch Caleb walk away to join the cleaning crew as they arrive, and I smile to myself.

I did not hire him to help, but he wants to help.

He painted my image without my permission, and somehow I just let him.

I have no time in my life for a man, but he's just…so much man that he made me find the time.

I was happy before. I was content. I had just the right kind of stress that I could handle.

Now, happy, content, and fulfilled don't even cut it. I'm burning to find out what happens next.

Epilogue

Five years later

Caleb

THE SUN IS SHINING on a crisp fall morning, and the peach trees I planted for Naomi five years ago are finally starting to produce.

I can see them from where I'm working this morning, freshening up the mural I painted on the inside of the fence separating the garden from the kitchen entrance.

One of the servers passes by on his way to work and stops to watch me.

"Cool," he says, nodding. "I like it."

The mural is pure chaos, with explosions of pink and orange. It's all inspired by that moment that Naomi and I shared that first day we met.

It's a bit too chaotic for the guests, but the kitchen staff likes it.

The aroma of honeysuckle and fresh coffee teases my nostrils, and I know who is sidling up behind me.

"Good morning, love." Of all the fantastic three-word phrases, that one might be my favorite. I smile as I drop my brushes and take my morning coffee in my hand and Naomi under my arm.

I love that she finds me, wherever I'm working, to bring me coffee every morning.

She presses a kiss to my forehead. "Good morning," I say, squeezing her tightly, demanding a deeper kiss.

She chuckles and pulls back. "Careful, don't spill."

"Can't help it. This fence makes me horny."

After five years, I still get hard whenever I see her, smell her, feel her skin against mine or hear her voice in my ear. This being her inn, she's pretty much everywhere.

I don't know if tree planting and general handyman work fall under the job description for an artist in residence. Then again, I don't think an artist in residence stays on for life.

As Naomi and I like to say, we make our own rules.

THE END

More by Abby Knox

Naughty Yachties

Shipped

Secret Baby on Board

Wrecked

Decked

Roped (coming soon!)

And plenty more on my Amazon page!

About the Author

Abby Knox writes feel-good, high-heat romance that she herself would want to read. Readers have described her stories as quirky, sexy, adorable, and hilarious. All of that adds up to Abby's overall goal in life: to be kind and to have fun!

Abby's favorite tropes include: Forced proximity, opposites attract, grumpy/sunshine, age gap, boss/employee, fated mates/insta-love, and more. Abby is heavily influenced by Buffy the Vampire Slayer, Gilmore Girls, and LOST. But don't worry, she won't ever make you suffer like Luke & Lorelai.

If any or all of that connects with you, then you came to the right place.

Join Abby's newsletter
and say hello at authorabbyknox@gmail.com

Made in the USA
Columbia, SC
07 July 2022